GILGAMESH AND ENKIDU

TRANSLATED BY N.K. SANDARS

PENGUIN BOOKS

PENGUIN BOOKS

Published by the Penguin Group
Penguin Books Ltd, 27 Wrights Lane, London w8 5TZ, England
Penguin Books USA Inc., 375 Hudson Street, New York, New York 10014, USA
Penguin Books Australia Ltd, Ringwood, Victoria, Australia
Penguin Books Canada Ltd, 10 Alcorn Avenue, Toronto, Ontario, Canada M4V 3B2
Penguin Books (NZ) Ltd, 182–190 Wairau Road, Auckland 10, New Zealand

Penguin Books Ltd, Registered Offices: Harmondsworth, Middlesex, England

These extracts are from *The Epic of Gilgamesh*, translated by N. K. Sandars,
first published in Penguin Classics 1960
This edition published 1995
1 3 5 7 9 10 8 6 4 2

Typeset by Rowland Phototypesetting Ltd, Bury St Edmunds, Suffolk
Printed in England by Clays Ltd, St Ives plc

CONTENTS

PROLOGUE
Gilgamesh King in Uruk

I will proclaim to the world the deeds of Gilgamesh. This was the man to whom all things were known; this was the king who knew the countries of the world. He was wise, he saw mysteries and knew secret things, he brought us a tale of the days before the flood. He went on a long journey, was weary, worn out with labour, returning he rested, he engraved on a stone the whole story.

When the gods created Gilgamesh they gave him a perfect body. Shamash the glorious sun endowed him with beauty, Adad the god of the storm endowed him with courage, the great gods made his beauty perfect, surpassing all others, terrifying like a great wild bull. Two thirds they made him god and one third man.

In Uruk he built walls, a great rampart, and the temple of blessed Eanna for the god of the firmament Anu, and for Ishtar the goddess of love. Look at it still today: the outer wall where the cornice runs, it shines with the brilliance of copper; and the inner wall, it has no equal. Touch the threshold, it is ancient. Approach Eanna the dwelling of Ishtar, our lady of love and war, the like of which no latter-day king, no man alive can equal. Climb upon the wall of Uruk; walk along it, I say; regard the foundation terrace and examine the masonry: is it not burnt brick and good? The seven sages laid the foundations.

The Coming of Enkidu

Gilgamesh went abroad in the world, but he met with none who could withstand his arms till he came to Uruk. But the men of Uruk muttered in their houses, 'Gilgamesh sounds the tocsin for his amusement, his arrogance has no bounds by day or night. No son is left with his father, for Gilgamesh takes them all, even the children; yet the king should be a shepherd to his people. His lust leaves no virgin to her lover, neither the warrior's daughter nor the wife of the noble; yet this is the shepherd of the city, wise, comely, and resolute.'

The gods heard their lament, the gods of heaven cried to the Lord of Uruk, to Anu the god of Uruk: 'A goddess made him, strong as a savage bull, none can withstand his arms. No son is left with his father, for Gilgamesh takes them all; and is this the king, the shepherd of his people? His lust leaves no virgin to her lover, neither the warrior's daughter nor the wife of the noble.' When

Anu had heard their lamentation the gods cried to Aruru, the goddess of creation, 'You made him, O Aruru, now create his equal; let it be as like him as his own reflection, his second self, stormy heart for stormy heart. Let them contend together and leave Uruk in quiet.'

So the goddess conceived an image in her mind, and it was of the stuff of Anu of the firmament. She dipped her hands in water and pinched off clay, she let it fall in the wilderness, and noble Enkidu was created. There was virtue in him of the god of war, of Ninurta himself. His body was rough, he had long hair like a woman's; it waved like the hair of Nisaba, the goddess of corn. His body was covered with matted hair like Samuqan's, the god of cattle. He was innocent of mankind; he knew nothing of the cultivated land.

Enkidu ate grass in the hills with the gazelle and lurked with wild beasts at the water-holes; he had joy of the water with the herds of wild game. But there was a trapper who met him one day face to face at the drinking-hole, for the wild game had entered his territory. On three days he met him face to face, and the trapper was frozen with fear. He went back to his house with the game that he had caught, and he was dumb, benumbed with terror. His face was altered like that of one who has made a long journey. With awe in his heart he spoke to his father: 'Father, there is a man, unlike any other, who comes down from the hills. He is the strongest in the world, he is like an immortal from heaven. He ranges over the hills with wild beasts and eats grass; he ranges through your land and comes down to the wells. I am afraid and dare not go near him. He fills in the pits which I dig and tears up my traps set for the game; he helps the beasts to escape and now they slip through my fingers.'

His father opened his mouth and said to the trapper, 'My son, in Uruk lives Gilgamesh; no one has ever prevailed against him, he is strong as a star from heaven. Go to Uruk, find Gilgamesh, extol the strength of this wild man. Ask him to give you a harlot, a wanton from the temple of love; return with her, and let her woman's power overpower this man. When next he comes down to drink at the wells she will be there, stripped naked; and when he sees her beckoning he will

5

embrace her, and then the wild beasts will reject him.'

So the trapper set out on his journey to Uruk and addressed himself to Gilgamesh saying, 'A man unlike any other is roaming now in the pastures; he is as strong as a star from heaven and I am afraid to approach him. He helps the wild game to escape; he fills in my pits and pulls up my traps.' Gilgamesh said, 'Trapper, go back, take with you a harlot, a child of pleasure. At the drinking-hole she will strip, and when he sees her beckoning he will embrace her and the game of the wilderness will surely reject him.'

Now the trapper returned, taking the harlot with him. After a three days' journey they came to the drinking-hole, and there they sat down; the harlot and the trapper sat facing one another and waited for the game to come. For the first day and for the second day the two sat waiting, but on the third day the herds came; they came down to drink and Enkidu was with them. The small wild creatures of the plains were glad of the water, and Enkidu with them, who ate grass with the gazelle and was born in the hills; and she saw him, the savage man, come from far-off in the hills. The trapper spoke to her: 'There he is. Now, woman, make your breasts bare, have no shame, do not delay but welcome his love. Let him see you naked, let him possess your body. When he comes near uncover yourself and lie with him; teach him, the savage man, your woman's art, for when he murmurs love to you the wild beasts that shared his life in the hills will reject him.'

She was not ashamed to take him, she made herself naked and welcomed his eagerness; as he lay on her murmuring love she taught him the woman's art. For six days and seven nights they lay together, for Enkidu had forgotten his home in the hills; but when he was satisfied he went back to the wild beasts. Then, when the gazelle saw him, they bolted away; when the wild creatures saw him they fled. Enkidu would have followed, but his body was bound as though with a cord, his knees gave way when he started to run, his swiftness was gone. And now the wild creatures had all fled away; Enkidu was grown weak, for wisdom was in him, and the thoughts of a man were in his heart. So he returned and sat down at the woman's feet, and listened intently to what she said. 'You are wise, Enkidu, and now you have become like a god. Why do you want to run wild with the beasts in the hills? Come with me. I will take you to strong-walled Uruk, to the blessed temple of Ishtar and of Anu, of love and of heaven: there Gilgamesh lives, who is very strong, and like a wild bull he lords it over men.'

When she had spoken Enkidu was pleased; he longed for a comrade, for one who would understand his heart. 'Come, woman, and take me to that holy temple, to the house of Anu and of Ishtar, and to the place where Gilgamesh lords it over the people. I will challenge him boldly, I will cry out aloud in Uruk, "I am the strongest here, I have come to change the old order, I am he who was born in the hills, I am he who is strongest of all."'

She said, 'Let us go, and let him see your face. I know very well where Gilgamesh is in great Uruk. O Enkidu, there all the people are dressed in their gorgeous robes, every day is holiday, the young men and the girls are wonderful to see. How sweet they smell! All the great ones are roused from their beds. O Enkidu, you who love life, I will show you Gilgamesh, a man of many moods; you shall look at him well in his radiant manhood. His body is perfect in strength and maturity; he never rests by night or day. He is stronger than you, so leave your boasting. Shamash the glorious sun has given favours to Gilgamesh, and Anu of the heavens, and Enlil, and Ea the wise has given him deep understanding. I tell you, even before you have left the wilderness, Gilgamesh will know in his dreams that you are coming.'

Now Gilgamesh got up to tell his dream to his mother, Ninsun, one of the wise gods. 'Mother, last night I had a dream. I was full of joy, the young heroes were round me and I walked through the night under the stars of the firmament, and one, a meteor of the stuff of Anu, fell down from heaven. I tried to lift it but it proved too heavy. All the people of Uruk came round to see it, the common people jostled and the nobles thronged to kiss its feet; and to me its attraction was like the love of woman. They helped me, I braced my forehead and I raised it with thongs and brought it to you, and you yourself pronounced it my brother.'

Then Ninsun, who is well-beloved and wise, said to Gilgamesh, 'This star of heaven which descended like a meteor from the sky; which you tried to lift, but found too heavy, when you tried to move it it would not budge, and so you brought it to my feet; I made it for you, a goad and spur, and you were drawn as though to a woman. This is the strong comrade, the one who brings help to his friend in his need. He is the strongest of wild creatures, the stuff of Anu; born in the grasslands and the wild hills reared him; when you see him you will be glad; you will love him as a woman and he will never forsake you. This is the meaning of the dream.'

Gilgamesh said, 'Mother, I dreamed a second dream. In the streets of strong-walled Uruk there lay an axe; the shape of it was strange and the people thronged round. I saw it and was glad. I bent down, deeply drawn towards it; I loved it like a woman and wore it at my side.' Ninsun answered, 'That axe, which you saw, which drew you so powerfully like love of a woman, that is the comrade whom I give you, and he will come in his strength like one of the host of heaven. He is the brave companion who rescues his friend in necessity.' Gilgamesh said to his mother, 'A friend, a counsellor has come to me from Enlil, and now I shall befriend and counsel him.' So Gilgamesh told his dreams; and the harlot retold them to Enkidu.

And now she said to Enkidu, 'When I look at you you have become like a god. Why do you yearn to run wild again with the beasts in the hills? Get up from the ground, the bed of a shepherd.' He listened to her words with care. It was good advice that she gave. She divided her clothing in two and with the one half she clothed him and with the other herself; and holding his hand she led him like a child to the sheepfolds, into the shepherds' tents. There all the shepherds crowded round to see him, they put down bread in front of him, but Enkidu could only suck the milk of wild animals. He fumbled and gaped, at a loss what to do or how he should eat the bread and drink the strong wine. Then the woman said, 'Enkidu, eat bread, it is the staff of life; drink the wine, it is the custom of the land.' So he ate till he was full and drank strong wine, seven goblets. He became merry, his heart exulted and his face shone. He rubbed down the matted hair of his body and anointed himself with oil. Enkidu had become a man; but when he had put on man's clothing he appeared like a bridegroom. He took arms to hunt the lion so that the shepherds could rest at night. He caught wolves and lions and the herdsmen lay down in peace; for Enkidu was their watchman, that strong man who had no rival.

He was merry living with the shepherds, till one day lifting his eyes he saw a man approaching. He said to the harlot, 'Woman, fetch that man here. Why has he come? I wish to know his name.' She went and called the man saying, 'Sir, where are you going on this weary journey?' The man answered, saying to Enkidu, 'Gilgamesh has gone into the marriage-house and shut out the people. He does strange things in Uruk, the city of great streets. At the roll of the drum work begins for the men, and work for the women. Gilgamesh the king is about to celebrate marriage with the Queen of Love, and he still demands to be first with the bride, the king to be first and the husband to follow, for that was ordained by the gods from his birth, from the time the umbilical cord was cut. But now the drums roll for the choice of the bride and the city groans.' At these words Enkidu turned white in the face. 'I will go to the place where Gilgamesh lords it over the people, I will challenge him boldly, and I will cry aloud in Uruk, "I have come to change the old order, for I am the strongest here."'

Now Enkidu strode in front and the woman followed behind. He entered Uruk, that great market, and all the folk thronged round him where he stood in the street in strong-walled Uruk. The people jostled; speaking of him they said, 'He is the spit of Gilgamesh.' 'He is shorter.' 'He is bigger of bone.' 'This is the one who was reared on the milk of wild beasts. His is the greatest strength.' The men rejoiced: 'Now Gilgamesh has met his match. This great one, this hero whose beauty is like a god, he is a match even for Gilgamesh.'

In Uruk the bridal bed was made, fit for the goddess of love. The bride waited for the bridegroom, but in the night Gilgamesh got up and came to the house. Then Enkidu stepped out, he stood in the street and blocked the way. Mighty Gilgamesh came on and Enkidu met him at the gate. He put out his foot and prevented Gilgamesh from entering the house, so they grappled, holding each other like bulls. They broke the doorposts and the walls shook, they snorted like bulls locked together. They shattered the doorposts and the walls shook. Gilgamesh bent his knee with his foot planted on the ground and with a turn Enkidu was thrown. Then immediately his fury died. When Enkidu was thrown he said to Gilgamesh, 'There is not another like you in the world. Ninsun, who is as strong as a wild ox in the byre, she was the mother who bore you, and now you are raised above all men, and Enlil has given you the kingship, for your strength surpasses the strength of men.' So Enkidu and Gilgamesh embraced and their friendship was sealed.

The Forest Journey

Enlil of the mountain, the father of the gods, had decreed the destiny of Gilgamesh. So Gilgamesh dreamed and Enkidu said, 'The meaning of the dream is this. The father of the gods has given you kingship, such is your destiny, everlasting life is not your destiny. Because of this do not be sad at heart, do not be grieved or oppressed. He has given you power to bind and to loose, to be the darkness and the light of mankind. He has given you unexampled supremacy over the people, victory in battle from which no fugitive returns, in forays and assaults from which there is no going back. But do not abuse this power, deal justly with your servants in the palace, deal justly before Shamash.'

The eyes of Enkidu were full of tears and his heart was sick. He sighed bitterly and Gilgamesh met his eye and said, 'My friend, why do you sigh so bitterly?' But Enkidu opened his mouth and said, 'I am weak, my arms have lost their strength, the cry of sorrow sticks in my throat, I am oppressed by idleness.' It was then that the lord Gilgamesh turned his thoughts to the Country of the Living; on the Land of Cedars the lord Gilgamesh reflected. He said to his servant Enkidu, 'I have not established my name stamped on bricks as my destiny decreed; therefore I will go to the country where the cedar is felled. I will set up my name in the place where the names of famous men are written, and where no man's name is written yet I will raise a monument to the gods. Because of the evil that is in the land, we will go to the forest and destroy the evil; for in the forest lives Humbaba whose name is "Hugeness", a ferocious giant.' But Enkidu sighed bitterly and said, 'When I went with the wild beasts ranging through the wilderness I discovered the forest; its length is ten thousand leagues in every direction. Enlil has appointed Humbaba to guard it and armed him in sevenfold terrors, terrible to all flesh is Humbaba. When he roars it is like the torrent of the storm, his breath is like fire, and his jaws are death itself. He guards the cedars so well that when the wild heifer stirs in the forest, though she is sixty leagues distant, he hears her. What man would willingly walk into that country and explore its depths? I tell you, weakness overpowers whoever goes near it: it is not an equal struggle when one fights with Humbaba; he is a great warrior, a battering-ram. Gilgamesh, the watchman of the forest never sleeps.'

Gilgamesh replied: 'Where is the man who can clamber to heaven? Only the gods live for ever with glorious Shamash, but as for us men, our days are numbered, our occupations are a breath of wind. How is this, already you are afraid! I will go first although I am your lord, and you may safely call out, "Forward, there is nothing to fear!" Then if I fall I leave behind me a name that endures; men will say of me, "Gilgamesh has fallen in fight with ferocious Humbaba." Long after the child has been born in my house, they will say it, and remember.' Enkidu spoke again to Gilgamesh, 'O my lord, if you will enter that country, go first to the hero Shamash, tell the Sun God, for the land is his. The country where the cedar is cut belongs to Shamash.'

Gilgamesh took up a kid, white without spot, and a brown one with it; he held them against his breast, and he carried them into the presence of the sun. He took in his hand his silver sceptre and he said to glorious Shamash, 'I am going to that country, O Shamash, I am going; my hands supplicate, so let it be well with my soul and bring me back to the quay of Uruk. Grant, I beseech, your protection, and let the omen be good.' Glorious Shamash answered, 'Gilgamesh, you are strong, but what is the Country of the Living to you?'

'O Shamash, hear me, hear me, Shamash, let my voice be heard. Here in the city man dies oppressed at heart, man perishes with despair in his heart. I have looked over the wall and I see the bodies floating on the river, and that will be my lot also. Indeed I know it is so, for whoever is tallest among men cannot reach the heavens, and the greatest cannot encompass the earth. Therefore I would enter that country: because I have not established my name stamped on brick as my destiny decreed, I will go to the country where the cedar is cut. I will set up my name where the names of famous men are written; and where no man's name is written I will raise a monument to the gods.' The tears ran down his face and he said, 'Alas, it is a long journey that I must take to the Land of Humbaba. If this enterprise is not to be accomplished, why did you move me, Shamash, with the restless desire to perform it? How can I succeed if you will not succour me? If I die in that country I will die without rancour, but if I return I will make a glorious offering of gifts and of praise to Shamash.'

So Shamash accepted the sacrifice of his tears; like the compassionate man he showed him mercy. He appointed strong allies for Gilgamesh, sons of one mother, and stationed them in the mountain caves. The great winds he appointed: the north wind, the whirlwind, the storm and the icy wind, the tempest and the scorching wind. Like vipers, like dragons, like a scorching fire, like a serpent that freezes the heart, a destroying flood and the lightning's fork, such were they and Gilgamesh rejoiced.

He went to the forge and said, 'I will give orders to the armourers; they shall cast us our weapons while we watch them.' So they gave orders to the armourers and the craftsmen sat down in conference. They went into the groves of the plain and cut willow and box-wood; they cast for them axes of nine score pounds, and great swords they cast with blades of six score pounds each one, with pommels and hilts of thirty pounds. They cast for Gilgamesh the axe 'Might of Heroes' and the bow of Anshan; and Gilgamesh was armed and Enkidu; and the weight of the arms they carried was thirty score pounds.

The people collected and the counsellors in the streets and in the market-place of Uruk; they came through the gate of seven bolts and Gilgamesh spoke to them in the market-place: 'I, Gilgamesh, go to see that creature of whom such things are spoken, the rumour of whose name fills the world. I will conquer him in his cedar wood and show the strength of the sons of Uruk, all the world shall know of it. I am committed to this enterprise: to climb the mountain, to cut down the cedar, and leave behind me an enduring name.' The counsellors of Uruk, the great market, answered him, 'Gilgamesh, you are young, your courage carries you too far, you cannot know what this enterprise means which you plan. We have heard that Humbaba is not like men who die, his weapons are such that none can stand against them; the forest stretches for ten thousand leagues in every direction; who would willingly go down to explore its depths? As for Humbaba, when he roars it is like the torrent of the storm, his breath is like fire and his jaws are death itself. Why do you crave to do this thing, Gilgamesh? It is no equal struggle when one fights with Humbaba, that battering-ram.'

When he heard these words of the counsellors Gilgamesh looked at his friend and laughed, 'How shall I answer them; shall I say I am afraid of Humbaba, I will sit at home all the rest of my days?' Then Gilgamesh opened his mouth again and said to Enkidu, 'My friend, let us go to the Great Palace, to Egalmah, and stand before Ninsun the queen. Ninsun is wise with deep knowledge, she will give us counsel for the road we must go.' They took each other by the hand as they went to Egalmah, and they went to Ninsun the great queen. Gilgamesh approached, he entered the palace and spoke to Ninsun. 'Ninsun, will you listen to me; I have a long journey to go, to the Land of Humbaba, I must travel an unknown road and fight a strange battle. From the day I go until I return, till I reach the cedar forest and destroy the evil which Shamash abhors, pray for me to Shamash.'

Ninsun went into her room, she put on a dress becoming to her body, she put on jewels to make her breast beautiful, she placed a tiara on her head and her skirts swept the ground. Then she went up to the altar of the Sun, standing upon the roof of the palace; she burnt incense and lifted her arms to Shamash as the smoke ascended: 'O Shamash, why did you give this restless heart to Gilgamesh, my son; why did you give it? You have moved him and now he sets out on a long journey to the Land of Humbaba, to travel an unknown road and fight a strange battle. Therefore from the day that he goes till the day he returns, until he reaches the cedar forest, until he kills Humbaba and destroys the evil thing which you, Shamash, abhor, do not forget him; but let the dawn, Aya, your dear bride, remind you always, and when day is done give him to the watchman of the night to keep him from harm.' Then Ninsun the mother of Gilgamesh extinguished the incense, and she called to Enkidu with this exhortation: 'Strong Enkidu, you are not the child of my body, but I will receive you as my adopted son; you are my other child like the foundlings they bring to the temple. Serve Gilgamesh as a foundling serves the temple and the priestess who reared him. In the presence of my women, my votaries and hierophants, I declare it.' Then she placed the amulet for a pledge round his neck, and she said to him, 'I entrust my son to you; bring him back to me safely.'

And now they brought to them the weapons, they put in their hands the great swords in their golden scabbards, and the bow and the quiver. Gilgamesh took the axe, he slung the quiver from his shoulder, and the bow of Anshan, and buckled the sword to his belt; and so they were armed and ready for the journey. Now all the people came and pressed on them and said, 'When will you return to the city?' The counsellors blessed Gilgamesh and warned him, 'Do not trust too much in your own strength, be watchful, restrain your blows at first. The one who goes in front protects his companion; the good guide who knows the way guards his friend. Let Enkidu lead the way, he knows the road to the forest, he has seen Humbaba and is experienced in battles; let him press first into the passes, let him be watchful and look to himself. Let Enkidu protect his friend, and guard his companion, and bring him safe through the pitfalls of the road. We, the counsellors of Uruk entrust our king to you, O Enkidu; bring him back safely to us.' Again to Gilgamesh they said, 'May Shamash give you your heart's desire, may he let you see with your eyes the thing accomplished which your lips have spoken; may he open a path for you where it is blocked, and a road for your feet to tread. May he open the mountains for your crossing, and may the night-time bring you the blessings of night, and Lugulbanda, your guardian god, stand beside you for victory. May you have victory in the battle as though you fought with a child. Wash your feet in the river of Humbaba to which you are journeying; in the evening dig a well, and let there always be pure water in your water-skin. Offer cold water to Shamash and do not forget Lugulbanda.'

Then Enkidu opened his mouth and said, 'Forward, there is nothing to fear. Follow me, for I know the place where Humbaba lives and the paths where he walks. Let the counsellors go back. Here is no cause for fear.' When the counsellors heard this they sped the hero on his way. 'Go, Gilgamesh, may your guardian god protect you on the road and bring you safely back to the quay of Uruk.'

After twenty leagues they broke their fast; after another thirty leagues they stopped for the night. Fifty leagues they walked in one day; in three days they had walked as much as a journey of a month and two weeks. They crossed seven mountains before they came to the gate of the forest. Then Enkidu called out to Gilgamesh, 'Do not go down into the forest; when I opened the gate my hand lost its strength.' Gilgamesh answered him, 'Dear friend, do not speak like a coward. Have we got the better of so many dangers and travelled so far, to turn back at last? You, who are tried in wars and battles, hold close to me now and you will feel no fear of death; keep beside me and your weakness will pass, the trembling will leave your hand. Would my friend rather stay behind? No, we will go down together into the heart of the forest. Let your courage be roused by the battle to come; forget death and follow me, a man resolute in action, but one who is not foolhardy. When two go together each will protect himself and shield his companion, and if they fall they leave an enduring name.'

Together they went down into the forest and they came to the green mountain. There they stood still, they were struck dumb; they stood still and gazed at the forest. They saw the height of the cedar, they saw the way into the forest and the track where Humbaba was used to walk. The way was broad and the going was good. They gazed at the mountain of cedars, the dwelling-place of the gods and the throne of Ishtar. The hugeness of the cedar rose in front of the mountain, its shade was beautiful, full of comfort; mountain and glade were green with brushwood.

There Gilgamesh dug a well before the setting sun. He went up the mountain and poured out fine meal on the ground and said, 'O mountain, dwelling of the gods, bring me a favourable dream.' Then they took each other by the hand and lay down to sleep; and sleep that flows from the night lapped over them. Gilgamesh dreamed, and at midnight sleep left him, and he told his dream to his friend. 'Enkidu, what was it that woke me if you did not? My friend, I have dreamed a dream. Get up, look at the mountain precipice. The sleep that the gods sent me is broken. Ah, my friend, what a dream I have had! Terror and confusion; I seized hold of a wild bull in the wilderness. It bellowed and beat up the dust till the whole sky was dark, my arm was seized and my tongue bitten. I fell back on my knee; then someone refreshed me with water from his water-skin.'

Enkidu said, 'Dear friend, the god to whom we are travelling is no wild bull, though his form is mysterious. That wild bull which you saw is Shamash the Protector; in our moment of peril he will take our hands. The one who gave water from his water-skin, that is your own god who cares for your good name, your Lugulbanda. United with him, together we will accomplish a work the fame of which will never die.'

Gilgamesh said, 'I dreamed again. We stood in a deep gorge of the mountain, and beside it we two were like the smallest of swamp flies; and suddenly the mountain fell, it struck me and caught my feet from under me. Then came an intolerable light blazing out, and in it was one whose grace and whose beauty were greater than the beauty of this world. He pulled me out from under the mountain, he gave me water to drink and my heart was comforted, and he set my feet on the ground.'

Then Enkidu the child of the plains said, 'Let us go down from the mountain and talk this thing over together.' He said to Gilgamesh the young god, 'Your dream is good, your dream is excellent, the mountain which you saw is Humbaba. Now, surely, we will seize and kill him, and throw his body down as the mountain fell on the plain.'

The next day after twenty leagues they broke their fast, and after another thirty they stopped for the night. They dug a well before the sun had set and Gilgamesh ascended the mountain. He poured out fine meal on the ground and said, 'O mountain, dwelling of the gods, send a dream for Enkidu, make him a favourable dream.' The mountain fashioned a dream for Enkidu; it came, an ominous dream; a cold shower passed over him, it caused him to cower like the mountain barley under a storm of rain. But Gilgamesh sat with his chin on his knees till the sleep which flows over all mankind lapped over him. Then, at midnight, sleep left him; he got up and said to his friend, 'Did you call me, or why did I wake? Did you touch me, or why am I terrified? Did not some god pass by, for my limbs are numb with fear? My friend, I saw a third dream and this dream was altogether frightful. The heavens roared and the earth roared again, daylight failed and darkness fell, lightnings flashed, fire blazed out, the clouds lowered, they rained down death. Then the brightness departed, the fire went out, and all was turned to ashes fallen about us. Let us go down from the mountain and talk this over, and consider what we should do.'

When they had come down from the mountain Gilgamesh seized the axe in his hand: he felled the cedar. When Humbaba heard the noise far off he was enraged; he cried out, 'Who is this that has violated my woods and cut down my cedar?' But glorious Shamash called to them out of heaven, 'Go forward, do not be afraid.' But now Gilgamesh was overcome by weakness, for sleep had seized him suddenly, a profound sleep held him; he lay on the ground, stretched out speechless, as though in a dream. When Enkidu touched him he did not rise, when he spoke to him he did not reply. 'O Gilgamesh, Lord of the plain of Kullab, the world grows dark, the shadows have spread over it, now is the glimmer of dusk. Shamash has departed, his bright head is quenched in the bosom of his mother Ningal. O Gilgamesh, how long will you lie like this, asleep? Never let the mother who gave you birth be forced in mourning into the city square.'

At length Gilgamesh heard him; he put on his breastplate, 'The Voice of Heroes', of thirty shekels' weight; he put it on as though it had been a light garment that he carried, and it covered him altogether. He straddled the earth like a bull that snuffs the ground and his teeth were clenched. 'By the life of my mother Ninsun who gave me birth, and by the life of my father, divine Lugulbanda, let me live to be the wonder of my mother, as when she nursed me on her lap.' A second time he said to him, 'By the life of Ninsun my mother who gave me birth, and by the life of my father, divine Lugulbanda, until we have fought this man, if man he is, this god, if god he is, the way that I took to the Country of the Living will not turn back to the city.'

Then Enkidu, the faithful companion, pleaded, answering him, 'O my lord, you do not know this monster and that is the reason you are not afraid. I who know him, I am terrified. His teeth are dragon's fangs, his countenance is like a lion, his charge is the rushing of the flood, with his look he crushes alike the trees of the forest and reeds in the swamp. O my Lord, you may go on if you choose into this land, but I will go back to the city. I will tell the lady your mother all your glorious deeds till she shouts for joy: and then I will tell the death that followed till she weeps for bitterness.' But Gilgamesh said, 'Immolation and sacrifice are not yet for me, the boat of the dead shall not go down, nor the three-ply cloth be cut for my shrouding. Not yet will my people be desolate, nor the pyre be lit in my house and my dwelling burnt on the fire. Today, give me your aid and you shall have mine: what then can go amiss with us two? All living creatures born of the flesh shall sit at last in the boat of the West, and when it sinks, when the boat of Magilum sinks, they are gone; but we shall go forward and fix our eyes on this monster. If your heart is fearful throw away fear; if there is terror in it throw away terror. Take your axe in your hand and attack. He who leaves the fight unfinished is not at peace.'

Humbaba came out from his strong house of cedar. Then Enkidu called out, 'O Gilgamesh, remember now your boasts in Uruk. Forward, attack, son of Uruk, there is nothing to fear.' When he heard these words his courage rallied; he answered, 'Make haste, close in, if the watchman is there do not let him escape to the woods where he will vanish. He has put on the first of his seven splendours but not yet the other six, let us trap him before he is armed.' Like a raging wild bull he snuffed the ground; the watchman of the woods turned full of threatenings, he cried out. Humbaba came from his strong house of cedar. He nodded his head and shook it, menacing Gilgamesh; and on him he fastened his eye, the eye of death. Then Gilgamesh called to Shamash and his tears were flowing, 'O glorious Shamash, I have followed the road you commanded but now if you send no succour how shall I escape?' Glorious Shamash heard his prayer and he summoned the great wind, the north wind, the whirlwind, the storm and the icy wind, the tempest and the scorching wind; they came like dragons, like a scorching fire, like a serpent that freezes the heart, a destroying flood and the lightning's fork. The eight winds rose up against Humbaba, they beat against his eyes; he was gripped, unable to go forward or back. Gilgamesh shouted, 'By the life of Ninsun my mother and divine Lugulbanda my father, in the Country of the Living, in this Land I have discovered your dwelling; my weak arms and my small weapons I have brought to this Land against you, and now I will enter your house.'

So he felled the first cedar and they cut the

branches and laid them at the foot of the mountain. At the first stroke Humbaba blazed out, but still they advanced. They felled seven cedars and cut and bound the branches and laid them at the foot of the mountain, and seven times Humbaba loosed his glory on them. As the seventh blaze died out they reached his lair. He slapped his thigh in scorn. He approached like a noble wild bull roped on the mountain, a warrior whose elbows are bound together. The tears started to his eyes and he was pale, 'Gilgamesh, let me speak. I have never known a mother, no, nor a father who reared me. I was born of the mountain, he reared me, and Enlil made me the keeper of this forest. Let me go free, Gilgamesh, and I will be your servant, you shall be my lord; all the trees of the forest that I tended on the mountain shall be yours. I will cut them down and build you a palace.' He took him by the hand and led him to his house, so that the heart of Gilgamesh was moved with compassion. He swore by the heavenly life, by the earthly life, by the underworld itself: 'O Enkidu, should not the snared bird return to its nest and the captive man return to his mother's arms?' Enkidu answered, 'The strongest of men will fall to fate if he has no judgement. Namtar, the evil fate that knows no distinction between men, will devour him. If the snared bird returns to its nest, if the captive man returns to his mother's arms, then you my friend will never return to the city where the mother is waiting who gave you birth. He will bar the mountain road against you, and make the pathways impassable.'

Humbaba said, 'Enkidu, what you have spoken is evil: you, a hireling, dependent for your bread! In envy and for fear of a rival you have spoken evil words.' Enkidu said, 'Do not listen, Gilgamesh: this Humbaba must die. Kill Humbaba first and his servants after.' But Gilgamesh said, 'If we touch him the blaze and the glory of light will be put out in confusion, the glory and glamour will vanish, its rays will be quenched.' Enkidu said to Gilgamesh, 'Not so, my friend. First entrap the bird, and where shall the chicks run then? Afterwards we can search out the glory and the glamour, when the chicks run distracted through the grass.'

Gilgamesh listened to the word of his companion, he took the axe in his hand, he drew the sword from his belt, and he struck Humbaba with a thrust of the sword to the neck, and Enkidu his comrade struck the second blow. At the third blow Humbaba fell. Then there followed confusion for this was the guardian of the forest whom they had felled to the ground. For as far as two leagues the cedars shivered when Enkidu felled the watcher of the forest, he at whose voice Hermon and Lebanon used to tremble. Now the mountains were moved and all the hills, for the guardian of the forest was killed. They attacked the cedars, the seven splendours of Humbaba were extinguished. So they pressed on into the forest bearing the sword of eight talents. They uncovered the sacred dwellings of the Anunnaki and while Gilgamesh felled the first of the trees of the forest Enkidu cleared their roots as far as the banks of Euphrates. They set Humbaba before the gods, before Enlil; they kissed the ground and dropped the shroud and set the head before him. When he saw the head of Humbaba, Enlil raged at them. 'Why did you do this thing? From henceforth may the fire be on your faces, may it eat the bread that you eat, may it drink where you drink.' Then Enlil took again the blaze and the seven splendours that had been Humbaba's: he gave the first to the river, and he gave to the lion, to the stone of execration, to the mountain and to the dreaded daughter of the Queen of Hell.

O Gilgamesh, king and conqueror of the dreadful blaze; wild bull who plunders the mountain, who crosses the sea, glory to him, and from the brave the greater glory is Enki's!

Ishtar and Gilgamesh, and the Death of Enkidu

Gilgamesh washed out his long locks and cleaned his weapons; he flung back his hair from his shoulders; he threw off his stained clothes and changed them for new. He put on his royal robes and made them fast. When Gilgamesh had put on the crown, glorious Ishtar lifted her eyes, seeing the beauty of Gilgamesh. She said, 'Come to me, Gilgamesh, and be my bridegroom; grant me seed of your body, let me be your bride and you shall be my husband. I will harness for you a chariot of lapis lazuli and of gold, with wheels of gold and horns of copper; and you shall have mighty demons of the storm for draft-mules. When you enter our house in the fragrance of cedar-wood, threshold and throne will kiss your feet. Kings, rulers, and princes will bow down before you; they shall bring you tribute from the mountains and the plain. Your ewes shall drop twins and your goats triplets; your pack-ass shall outrun mules; your oxen shall have no rivals, and your chariot horses shall be famous far-off for their swiftness.'

Gilgamesh opened his mouth and answered glorious Ishtar, 'If I take you in marriage, what gifts can I give in return? What ointments and clothing for your body? I would gladly give you bread and all sorts of food fit for a god. I would give you wine to drink fit for a queen. I would pour out barley to stuff your granary; but as for making you my wife – that I will not. How would it go with me? Your lovers have found you like a brazier which smoulders in the cold, a back door which keeps out neither squall of wind nor storm, a castle which crushes the garrison, pitch that blackens the bearer, a water-skin that chafes the carrier, a stone which falls from the parapet, a battering-ram turned back from the enemy, a sandal that trips the wearer. Which of your lovers did you ever love for ever? What shepherd of yours has pleased you for all time? Listen to me while I tell the tale of your lovers. There was Tammuz, the lover of your youth, for him you decreed wailing, year after year. You loved the many-coloured roller, but still you struck and broke his wing; now in the grove he sits and cries, "Kappi, kappi, my wing, my wing." You have loved the lion tremendous in strength: seven pits you dug for him, and seven. You have loved the stallion magnificent in battle, and for him you decreed whip and spur and a thong, to gallop seven leagues by force and to muddy the water before he drinks; and for his mother Silili lamentations. You have loved the shepherd of the flock; he made meal-cake for you day after day, he killed kids for your sake. You struck and turned him into a wolf; now his own herd-boys chase him away, his own hounds worry his flanks. And did you not love Ishullanu, the gardener of your father's palmgrove? He brought you baskets filled with dates without end; every day he loaded your table. Then you turned your eyes on him and said, "Dearest Ishullanu, come here to me, let us enjoy your manhood, come forward and take me, I am yours." Ishullanu answered, "What are you asking from me? My mother has baked and I have eaten; why should I come to such as you for food that is tainted and rotten? For when was a screen of rushes sufficient protection from frosts?" But when you had heard his answer you struck him. He was changed to a blind mole deep in the earth, one whose desire is always beyond his reach. And if you and I should be lovers, should not I be served in the same fashion as all these others whom you loved once?'

When Ishtar heard this she fell into a bitter rage, she went up to high heaven. Her tears poured down in front of her father Anu, and Antum her mother. She said, 'My father, Gilgamesh has heaped insults on me, he has told over all my abominable behaviour, my foul and hideous acts.' Anu opened his mouth and said, 'Are you a father of gods? Did you not quarrel with Gilgamesh the king, so now he has related your abominable behaviour, your foul and hideous acts?'

Ishtar opened her mouth and said again, 'My father, give me the Bull of Heaven to destroy Gilgamesh. Fill Gilgamesh, I say, with arrogance to his destruction; but if you refuse to give me the Bull of Heaven I will break in the doors of hell and smash the bolts; there will be confusion of people, those above with those from the lower depths. I shall bring up the dead to eat food like the living; and the hosts of dead will outnumber the living.' Anu said to great Ishtar, 'If I do what you desire there will be seven years of drought throughout Uruk when corn will be seedless husks. Have you saved grain enough for the people and grass for the cattle?' Ishtar replied, 'I have saved grain for the people, grass for the cattle; for seven years of seedless husks there is grain and there is grass enough.'

When Anu heard what Ishtar had said he gave her the Bull of Heaven to lead by the halter down to Uruk. When they reached the gates of Uruk the Bull went to the river; with his first snort cracks opened in the earth and a hundred young men fell down to death. With his second snort cracks opened and two hundred fell down to death. With his third snort cracks opened, Enkidu doubled over but instantly recovered, he dodged aside and leapt on the Bull and seized it by the horns. The Bull of Heaven foamed in his face, it brushed him with the thick of its tail. Enkidu cried to Gilgamesh, 'My friend, we boasted that we would leave enduring names behind us. Now thrust in your sword between the nape and the horns.' So Gilgamesh followed the Bull, he seized the thick of its tail, he thrust the sword between the nape and the horns and slew the Bull. When they had killed the Bull of Heaven they cut out its heart and gave it to Shamash, and the brothers rested.

But Ishtar rose up and mounted the great wall of Uruk; she sprang on to the tower and uttered a curse: 'Woe to Gilgamesh, for he has scorned me in killing the Bull of Heaven.' When Enkidu heard these words he tore out the Bull's right thigh and tossed it in her face saying, 'If I could lay my hands on you, it is this I should do to you, and lash the entrails to your side.'. Then Ishtar called together her people, the dancing and singing girls, the prostitutes of the temple, the courtesans. Over the thigh of the Bull of Heaven she set up lamentation.

But Gilgamesh called the smiths and the armourers, all of them together. They admired the immensity of the horns. They were plated with lapis lazuli two fingers thick. They were thirty pounds each in weight, and their capacity in oil was six measures, which he gave to his guardian god, Lugulbanda. But he carried the horns into the palace and hung them on the wall. Then they washed their hands in Euphrates, they embraced each other and went away. They drove through the streets of Uruk where the heroes were gathered to see them, and Gilgamesh called to the singing girls, 'Who is most glorious of the heroes, who is most eminent among men?' 'Gilgamesh is the most glorious of heroes, Gilgamesh is most eminent among men.' And now there was feasting, and celebrations and joy in the palace, till the heroes lay down saying, 'Now we will rest for the night.'

When the daylight came Enkidu got up and cried to Gilgamesh, 'O my brother, such a dream I had last night. Anu, Enlil, Ea and heavenly Shamash took counsel together, and Anu said to Enlil, "Because they have killed the Bull of Heaven, and because they have killed Humbaba who guarded the Cedar Mountain one of the two must die." Then glorious Shamash answered the hero Enlil, "It was by your command they killed the Bull of Heaven, and killed Humbaba, and must Enkidu die although innocent?" Enlil flung round in rage at glorious Shamash, "You dare to say this, you who went about with them every day like one of themselves!"'

So Enkidu lay stretched out before Gilgamesh; his tears ran down in streams and he said to Gilgamesh, 'O my brother, so dear as you are to me, brother, yet they will take me from you.' Again he said, 'I must sit down on the threshold of the dead and never again will I see my dear brother with my eyes.'

While Enkidu lay alone in his sickness he cursed the gate as though it was living flesh, 'You there, wood of the gate, dull and insensible, witless, I searched for you over twenty leagues until I saw the towering cedar. There is no wood like you in our land. Seventy-two cubits high and twenty-four wide, the pivot and the ferrule and the jambs are perfect. A master craftsman from Nippur has made you; but O, if I had known the conclusion! If I had known that this was all the good that would come of it, I would have raised the axe and split you into little pieces and set up here a gate

of wattle instead. Ah, if only some future king
had brought you here, or some god had fashioned
you. Let him obliterate my name and write his
own, and the curse fall on him instead of on
Enkidu.'

With the first brightening of dawn Enkidu
raised his head and wept before the Sun God, in
the brilliance of the sunlight his tears streamed
down. 'Sun God, I beseech you, about that vile
Trapper, that Trapper of nothing because of
whom I was to catch less than my comrade; let
him catch least, make his game scarce, make him
feeble, taking the smaller of every share, let his
quarry escape from his nets.'

When he had cursed the Trapper to his heart's
content he turned on the harlot. He was roused
to curse her also. 'As for you, woman, with a great
curse I curse you! I will promise you a destiny to
all eternity. My curse shall come on you soon
and sudden. You shall be without a roof for your
commerce, for you shall not keep house with
other girls in the tavern, but do your business in
places fouled by the vomit of the drunkard. Your
hire will be potter's earth, your thievings will be

flung into the hovel, you will sit at the cross-roads in the dust of the potter's quarter, you will make your bed on the dunghill at night, and by day take your stand in the wall's shadow. Brambles and thorns will tear your feet, the drunk and the dry will strike your cheek and your mouth will ache. Let you be stripped of your purple dyes, for I too once in the wilderness with my wife had all the treasure I wished.'

When Shamash heard the words of Enkidu he called to him from heaven: 'Enkidu, why are you cursing the woman, the mistress who taught you to eat bread fit for gods and drink wine of kings? She who put upon you a magnificent garment, did she not give you glorious Gilgamesh for your companion, and has not Gilgamesh, your own brother, made you rest on a royal bed and recline on a couch at his left hand? He has made the princes of the earth kiss your feet, and now all the people of Uruk lament and wail over you. When you are dead he will let his hair grow long for your sake, he will wear a lion's pelt and wander through the desert.'

When Enkidu heard glorious Shamash his

angry heart grew quiet, he called back the curse and said, 'Woman, I promise you another destiny. The mouth which cursed you shall bless you! Kings, princes and nobles shall adore you. On your account a man though twelve miles off will clap his hand to his thigh and his hair will twitch. For you he will undo his belt and open his treasure and you shall have your desire; lapis lazuli, gold and carnelian from the heap in the treasury. A ring for your hand and a robe shall be yours. The priest will lead you into the presence of the gods. On your account a wife, a mother of seven, was forsaken.'

As Enkidu slept alone in his sickness, in bitterness of spirit he poured out his heart to his friend. 'It was I who cut down the cedar, I who levelled the forest, I who slew Humbaba and now see what has become of me. Listen, my friend, this is the dream I dreamed last night. The heavens roared, and earth rumbled back an answer; between them stood I before an awful being, the sombre-faced man-bird; he had directed on me his purpose. His was a vampire face, his foot was a lion's foot, his hand was an eagle's talon. He fell on me and his claws were in my hair, he held me fast and I smothered; then he transformed me so that my arms became wings covered with feathers. He turned his stare towards me, and he led away to the palace of Irkalla, the Queen of Darkness, to the house from which none who enters ever returns, down the road from which there is no coming back.

'There is the house whose people sit in darkness; dust is their food and clay their meat. They are clothed like birds with wings for covering, they see no light, they sit in darkness. I entered the house of dust and I saw the kings of the earth, their crowns put away for ever; rulers and princes, all those who once wore kingly crowns and ruled the world in the days of old. They who had stood in the place of the gods like Anu and Enlil, stood now like servants to fetch baked meats in the house of dust, to carry cooked meat and cold water from the water-skin. In the house of dust which I entered were high priests and acolytes, priests of the incantation and of ecstasy; there were servers of the temple, and there was Etana, that king of Kish whom the eagle carried to heaven in the days of old. I saw also Samuqan, god of cattle, and there was Ereshkigal the Queen of the Underworld; and Belit-Sheri squatted in front of her, she who is recorder of the gods and keeps the books of death. She held a tablet from which she read. She raised her head, she saw me and spoke: "Who has brought this one here?" Then I awoke like a man drained of blood who wanders alone in a waste of rushes; like one whom the bailiff has seized and his heart pounds with terror.'

Gilgamesh had peeled off his clothes, he listened to his words and wept quick tears, Gilgamesh listened and his tears flowed. He opened his mouth and spoke to Enkidu: 'Who is there in strong-walled Uruk who has wisdom like this? Strange things have been spoken, why does your heart speak strangely? The dream was marvellous but the terror was great; we must treasure the dream whatever the terror; for the dream has shown that misery comes at last to the healthy man, the end of life is sorrow.' And Gilgamesh lamented, 'Now I will pray to the great gods, for my friend had an ominous dream.'

This day on which Enkidu dreamed came to an

end and he lay stricken with sickness. One whole day he lay on his bed and his suffering increased. He said to Gilgamesh, the friend on whose account he had left the wilderness, 'Once I ran for you, for the water of life, and I now have nothing.' A second day he lay on his bed and Gilgamesh watched over him but the sickness increased. A third day he lay on his bed, he called out to Gilgamesh, rousing him up. Now he was weak and his eyes were blind with weeping. Ten days he lay and his suffering increased, eleven and twelve days he lay on his bed of pain. Then he called to Gilgamesh, 'My friend, the great goddess cursed me and I must die in shame. I shall not die like a man fallen in battle; I feared to fall, but happy is the man who falls in the battle, for I must die in shame.' And Gilgamesh wept over Enkidu. With the first light of dawn he raised his voice and said to the counsellors of Uruk:

'Hear me, great ones of Uruk,
I weep for Enkidu, my friend,
Bitterly moaning like a woman mourning
I weep for my brother.
O Enkidu, my brother,

You were the axe at my side,
My hand's strength, the sword in my belt,
The shield before me,
A glorious robe, my fairest ornament;
An evil Fate has robbed me.
The wild ass and the gazelle
That were father and mother,
All long-tailed creatures that nourished you
Weep for you,
All the wild things of the plain and pastures;
The paths that you loved in the forest of cedars
Night and day murmur.
Let the great ones of strong-walled Uruk
Weep for you;
Let the finger of blessing
Be stretched out in mourning;
Enkidu, young brother. Hark,
There is an echo through all the country
Like a mother mourning.
Weep all the paths where we walked together;
And the beasts we hunted, the bear and hyena,
Tiger and panther, leopard and lion,
The stag and the ibex, the bull and the doe.
The river along whose banks we used to walk,
Weeps for you,
Ula of Elam and dear Euphrates

Where once we drew water for the water-skins.
The mountain we climbed where we slew the
 Watchman,
Weeps for you.
The warriors of strong-walled Uruk
Where the Bull of Heaven was killed,
Weep for you.
All the people of Eridu
Weep for you Enkidu.
Those who brought grain for your eating
Mourn for you now;
Who rubbed oil on your back
Mourn for you now;
Who poured beer for your drinking
Mourn for you now.
The harlot who anointed you with fragrant ointment
Laments for you now;
The women of the palace, who brought you a wife,
A chosen ring of good advice,
Lament for you now.
And the young men your brothers
As though they were women
Go long-haired in mourning.
What is this sleep which holds you now?
You are lost in the dark and cannot hear me.'

He touched his heart but it did not beat, nor did he lift his eyes again. When Gilgamesh touched his heart it did not beat. So Gilgamesh laid a veil, as one veils the bride, over his friend. He began to rage like a lion, like a lioness robbed of her whelps. This way and that he paced round the bed, he tore out his hair and strewed it around. He dragged off his splendid robes and flung them down as though they were abominations.

In the first light of dawn Gilgamesh cried out, 'I made you rest on a royal bed, you inclined on a couch at my left hand, the princes of the earth kissed your feet. I will cause all the people of Uruk to weep over you and raise the dirge of the dead. The joyful people will stoop with sorrow; and when you have gone to the earth I will let my hair grow long for your sake, I will wander through the wilderness in the skin of a lion.' The next day also, in the first light, Gilgamesh lamented; seven days and seven nights he wept for Enkidu, until the worm fastened on him. Only then he gave him up to the earth, for the Anunnaki, the judges, had seized him.

Then Gilgamesh issued a proclamation through

the land, he summoned them all, the copper-smiths, the goldsmiths, the stone-workers, and commanded them, 'Make a statue of my friend.' The statue was fashioned with a great weight of lapis lazuli for the breast and of gold for the body. A table of hard-wood was set out, and on it a bowl of carnelian filled with honey, and a bowl of lapis lazuli filled with butter. These he exposed and offered to the Sun; and weeping he went away.

Glossary of Names

ARURU: a goddess of creation, creator of Enkidu

Bull of Heaven: a personification of drought created by Anu for Ishtar

EA: god of the sweet waters, also of wisdom, patron of arts and one of the creators of mankind

ENLIL: god of earth, wind and the universal air, ultimately spirit; the executive of Anu

ERESHKIGAL/IRKALLA: Queen of the Underworld, a counterpart of Persephone

ISHTAR: goddess of love and fertility, also a goddess of war, called the Queen of Heaven

LUGULBANDA: a king of Uruk, god and shepherd, protector of Gilgamesh

NINSUN: mother of Gilgamesh, a minor goddess noted for wisdom

SHAMASH: the sun

PENGUIN 60s CLASSICS

READ MORE IN PENGUIN

For complete information about books available from Penguin and how to order them, please write to us at the appropriate address below. Please note that for copyright reasons the selection of books varies from country to country.

IN THE UNITED KINGDOM: Please write to *Dept. EP, Penguin Books Ltd, Bath Road, Harmondsworth, Middlesex UB7 0DA.*

IN THE UNITED STATES: Please write to *Consumer Sales, Penguin USA, P.O. Box 999, Dept. 17109, Bergenfield, New Jersey 07621-0120.* VISA and MasterCard holders call 1-800-253-6476 to order Penguin titles.

IN CANADA: Please write to *Penguin Books Canada Ltd, 10 Alcorn Avenue, Suite 300, Toronto, Ontario M4V 3B2.*

IN AUSTRALIA: Please write to *Penguin Books Australia Ltd, P.O. Box 257, Ringwood, Victoria 3134.*

IN NEW ZEALAND: Please write to *Penguin Books (NZ) Ltd, Private Bag 102902, North Shore Mail Centre, Auckland 10.*

IN INDIA: Please write to *Penguin Books India Pvt Ltd, 706 Eros Apartments, 56 Nehru Place, New Delhi 110 019.*

IN THE NETHERLANDS: Please write to *Penguin Books Netherlands bv, Postbus 3507, NL-1001 AH Amsterdam.*

IN GERMANY: Please write to *Penguin Books Deutschland GmbH, Metzlerstrasse 26, 60594 Frankfurt am Main.*

IN SPAIN: Please write to *Penguin Books S. A., Bravo Murillo 19, 1° B, 28015 Madrid.*

IN ITALY: Please write to *Penguin Italia s.r.l., Via Felice Casati 20, I–20124 Milano.*

IN FRANCE: Please write to *Penguin France S. A., 17 rue Lejeune, F–31000 Toulouse.*

IN JAPAN: Please write to *Penguin Books Japan, Ishikiribashi Building, 2–5–4, Suido, Bunkyo-ku, Tokyo 112.*

IN GREECE: Please write to *Penguin Hellas Ltd, Dimocritou 3, GR–106 71 Athens.*

IN SOUTH AFRICA: Please write to *Longman Penguin Southern Africa (Pty) Ltd, Private Bag X08, Bertsham 2013.*